Dedicated to

ELIZABETH, CAROL, CLAIRE, LOUISE AND KERRIE

THE *Sacred* CAT

© 1998 MARIE STUTTARD AND DENESE MOORE.

PUBLISHED 1998 BY SACRED CAT LIMITED

PO BOX 25-667, AUCKLAND

NEW ZEALAND

E-MAIL: INFO@SACREDCAT.CO.NZ

HOME PAGE AT HTTP://WWW.SACREDCAT.CO.NZ/

ISBN: 0-473-05171-0

LIMITED EDITION FIRST PRINTING

THE Sacred CAT

Written by Marie Stuttard

Photographs by Denese Moore

Lao-Tsun was only a kitten when he learned that his Birman ancestors were the Sacred Cats of Burma.

A legend about them and how they became Sacred Cats had been told by one generation of Birmans to another for centuries. However, many questions remained unanswered.

PROLOGUE

He had a passionate desire to know if there were still Sacred Cats in the underground Temple of Lao-Tsun, after which he had been named. He also had to confirm his belief that he was being guided by his ancestor, Sinh, around whom the legend was born.

$\mathcal{E}$VEN AS A KITTEN I HAD A DREAM. I DREAMED I would travel the world to find the home of my ancestors in Burma. In my innocence, I didn't realise what a long and perilous journey it would be, but youth plunges into adventure with little thought of danger. I certainly never thought of it. When I left home I had no idea what lay ahead yet there were many times when the

THE DREAM

journey nearly ended in disaster. It was only my conviction that I was being guided by Sinh that gave me the will and the determination to try to make my dream come true.

When I was little, I was just like other kittens. I loved being with my brothers and sisters. We were full of energy, exuberance and curiosity and played together from early morning until dusk, stopping only to eat and sleep. We were in a timeless world of fun and fantasy.

One day while playing a game with them, I felt a need to be by myself. Creeping into the bushes nearby I sat there feeling uncertain why I had come. After a while I became restless and was about to leave when a calmness enveloped me that was so soothing I found myself wishing I did not have to go back.

After that experience, although I still enjoyed play, I preferred to be on my own. I found a special place among the branches of a tree where I could sit by myself... and think. Such a sense of peace came over me in that quiet place, it made me wonder about my life and why I was not like other cats.

Each time, the feeling that I was different became stronger. My thoughts kept revolving around the question, "Why am I different?" Had it something to do with my breed? I knew I was a Birman. My father had told me so, but what Birmans were and how we were different from other cats I didn't know.

My question was answered one day when our father, Li Ming, a large and dignified cat, called all of us to him. "I have something important to tell you," he said seriously. As we sat waiting, I wondered if what we would hear from our father would explain the puzzle within me.

After a moment's silence Li Ming began to speak, slowly at first and then with an emotion we had never heard before. "The time has come for me to tell you about our ancestors," he said. "We... are... Birmans."

In a loud whisper my brother, Irra, said, "We know that!" Our mother, Karissima, looked at him sharply. Irra bowed his head.

Father continued, "In legend, we are the Sacred Cats of Burma."

At the mention of "Sacred Cats", my heart beat more quickly. Did Sacred Cats feel different too? "Where is Burma?" I asked.

"Far, far away," Li Ming replied.

"How far away?"

"Let your father tell his story," Karissima said sternly.

"Before the time of Buddha," Li Ming said proudly, "one hundred Birmans lived in an underground temple dedicated to a golden goddess with sapphire-blue eyes called Tsun-Kyan-Tse. The priests in the temple worshipped us and treated us as gods."

My brothers and sisters began to fidget but I listened intently, anxious to hear every word, then asked, "Why did they worship us, Father?"

"Shhh!" said my mother.

"Just listen," ordered Li Ming. "One night raiders attacked the temple and killed the head priest, Mun-ha, as he knelt before the goddess. His cat, Sinh, immediately jumped onto the body of his dead master and defied the robbers, inspiring the priests to do the same." Li Ming's face reflected the pride he felt for his ancestor. "At that moment, Mun-Ha's soul entered his cat and as it did so, the power of the goddess changed Sinh." Li Ming looked at me. "Yes, Lao-Tsun, the goddess changed Sinh's yellow eyes to sapphire-blue like her own. His white fur became golden and his face, ears, tail and legs turned the colour of earth, but his paws... " he stopped for a moment, then said slowly, "his paws, which had touched his master, remained white as a symbol of purity!"

One by one the others had slipped away, but my father's telling of the legend kept me spellbound. "What happened next?"

"Sinh stayed in front of the goddess for seven days and seven nights." Li Ming's eyes had a far-away look. "Then... he died."

I was shocked. "He died!"

My father looked at me kindly. "Don't despair, Lao-Tsun", he said, "for when Sinh died, he went to paradise, taking Mun-Ha's soul with him."

"What is paradise, Father?"

"It's a place of supreme happiness," Li Ming said, then explained what happened next. "When the priests assembled to choose a successor, a horn sounded and all the temple cats appeared - each one changed to Sinh's colouring! Ever since that time," he said joyfully, "all Birmans have looked like Sinh."

"Do I look like Sinh?"

"Yes," replied my father, "we all do."

"But our fur isn't golden," I said.

"It was a long time ago," was all Li Ming could say,

"but, Lao-Tsun, we have sapphire-blue eyes too. And look at your paws - see how white they are against the earth colour of your legs, just like Sinh's!"

Looking at my paws, which I'd never noticed before, I was amazed to find that they were indeed pure white - just as my father had said.

"Because we look like Sinh," Li Ming went on, "this means we are very special cats!"

Fascinated by what I had heard, I began to feel special too. The Sacred Cats! The more I thought about them, the more there was a kinship with my ancestors.

"Are there still Sacred Cats, the descendants of Sinh, in Burma now? Do they live in the temple? Could I go to paradise to be with Sinh?" I demanded, overwhelmed by all my father had told me.

Li Ming had to admit he didn't know. "Every Birman father for generations has passed on the legend of the

Sacred Cats to his family, exactly as it had been told to him," he said. "In this way, no matter where they live, Birmans always revere their ancestors."

Li Ming looked down at me and said, "Lao-Tsun, I want you not only to honour our ancestors but be proud that you are called after the temple itself. Your name means, 'The Dwelling Place of the Gods'."

I stared at my father with awe. I was called after the temple! The legend now took on an even greater meaning and my belief in it deepened.

For the first time in my life I became really excited and rushed around telling every cat the meaning of my name and about the legend. "The Birman is a wonderful breed!" I boasted to our neighbours.

They were not impressed. A wild cat called me a snob, another laughed. The others ignored me. I sighed. "Nobody understands."

I found it particularly difficult to accept that members of my own family, even my favourite sister, Saraha, were not interested in the legend. This upset me. I yearned to share what I had learned with everyone, especially those closest to me. But it meant nothing to them.

I fretted and worried that I wasn't worthy of spreading the news about our ancestors. That thought

made me feel unsettled and unsure of myself. Washing my fur with short, angry licks, I tried to cleanse myself of feelings of self-doubt.

One morning everything changed. As the soft light of dawn was breaking, I slipped away from my sleeping family.

The air was exceptionally still. The rising sun patterned the sky with delicate tints of pink and white. I was filled with a sense of exhilaration and delight. High above me, birds were singing and in the distance a cock crowed. The energy of the new day was all around me.

I sat among the branches of my favourite tree, absorbing the sights and sounds. From nowhere came a bolt of light that dazed me with its intensity. My fur rose and I tensed. Arching my back in fear, I hissed. Suddenly the air around me began to vibrate and a wave of contentment flowed through me. Then the contentment gradually turned into a happiness I had never experienced before. I relaxed completely and slipped into a sleep that was as deep as it was dreamless.

Conscious of nothing until the hot midday sun filtered through the branches above me, I awoke and tried to unravel the meaning of my experience. The more I thought, the more confused I became but I was determined to discover the reason behind it. Breaking into my thoughts a voice called, "Oh, there you are, Lao-Tsun. I've been searching everywhere for you. Come and play!" Saraha climbed the tree and sat beside me.

I loved her dearly but at that moment I was in no mood for company and wished only to be alone. But

she wouldn't give up, so reluctantly I did as she wanted and ran with her.

"Did you see a great light this morning, Saraha?" I inquired as we came close to the clearing where our brothers and sisters were having a game. She gazed at me blankly and I knew she had not. A thought came to me. What had happened was meant only for me.

Another day she asked, "What are you thinking, Lao-Tsun?"

I looked at her. She seemed really interested. Slowly I said, "I keep wondering, Saraha, 'Who am I?' - but I can't find an answer."

"I know who you are," she replied brightly, "you're the son of Li Ming and you're my brother."

"I know that," I said with a laugh, "but who am I in another sense?"

She didn't understand. "What do you mean?"

I tried to explain. "You see, Saraha, I'm sure there's more to life than just play... " My words made no sense to her and with a sigh she rushed away to be with the crowd again. I felt rejected and my feeling of isolation

grew. There was no one I could talk to or confide in.

Trying to heal the hurt, I sat quietly for a long time and thought about my ancestor. I wondered what he would have done. The more I thought about him, the more I seemed to be aware of myself.

Without warning, a flash of brilliant blue light swept across my eyes. It came so suddenly, for a moment I couldn't move, even though in fright I tried to run away. The glow of the light increased until it enveloped my whole body. I cried out in alarm but there was no one to hear my call. The light turned to warmth and gradually all trace of fear left me. I could feel myself purring with a deep contentment and became conscious of an overwhelming presence all around. I knew I was not alone.

A surge of energy shot up my spine. It seemed to explode within my head. I didn't try to fight it – I couldn't. I just lay there, aware of myself as never before. It was as though my mind and my body were flowing together like a great river and I was conscious only of a state of wonderment.

Suddenly I knew that my ancestor was beside me and I was overcome with a feeling of great happiness. In that instant I dedicated my life to Sinh.

Another blaze of light surrounded me and I knew my vow had been accepted. Returning to my family, I decided no one should know of my dedication.

My need to find out more about Sinh and the Sacred Cats grew more intense, but all Li Ming knew was what had been told to him by his father. An urgency possessed me. Day after day I was filled with an increasing desire to leave home and search for an answer.

THE *Sacred* CAT

22

It was then I had my dream.

I dreamed I would travel the world to Burma.

I dreamed I would find the Temple of Lao-Tsun and the Sacred Cats.

I dreamed I would prove the legend of Sinh to be true.

My father was shocked when I told him of my dream.

"You go to Burma!" Li Ming exclaimed in astonishment. "You couldn't do that!"

"Why not?" I demanded, upset that my father had so little faith in me.

"You're too small... too young... you don't even know where Burma is." Li Ming looked at me, then began to laugh. "You're foolish," he said, "absolutely foolish to think that a little cat from nowhere could find the descendants of our sacred ancestor."

"I will do it," I said stubbornly, "and when I get to Burma I may even become a Sacred Cat myself."

"I don't want to hear any more talk like this," Li Ming said firmly, "and I will not have you mocking the legend."

"I'm not mocking the legend," I protested. "I believe in it. But I must go to Burma to prove that it is true."

Angry and upset, Li Ming turned his back on me and walked away. I was dispirited – but defiant for I knew that nothing would stop me.

When word got round that I wanted to become a Sacred Cat, I was the butt of jeers and abuse.

"Who does he think he is?" snarled a large ginger tom in my hearing. "Why, I could break him in half with one paw!"

"Lao-Tsun a Sacred Cat?" said a tortoiseshell cat scathingly. "What a joke!"

Although resenting their attitude, I realised I would have to become much stronger, so part of my plan was to become very strong indeed. No matter what cruel things they said to me, I went on quietly and methodically with my preparations, always with the conviction that my ancestor was watching over me.

Every day I would run, further and further from home until I was exhausted. After a short rest, I would push myself to maintain the same pace on the journey back. Soon I could out-run my brothers and sisters, leaving them far behind. Each night I would droop with weariness but each morning I was up again to continue this punishing schedule according to my plan.

Never satisfied, I stepped up my training. Over and over again I would aim for the highest point of a tall tree and race up its trunk in less and less time.

"Why?" Saraha asked one day after I'd nearly fallen from a top branch. "Why put yourself in danger, Lao-Tsun? There's no pleasure in that."

"Where I'm going," I explained, "pleasure does not come into it. My purpose is to find the Temple of Lao-Tsun, the dwelling place of our ancestors."

With a flick of her tail, Saraha said, "Well, I think it's all quite ridiculous."

"Don't tread on my dream, Saraha," I warned.

Saraha stared at me and saw the determination in my eyes. "No," she said quietly, "I would never do that, Lao-Tsun, for deep down, I do believe in you." Her words gave me courage.

Water fascinated me. I waded regularly into a nearby river and battled its strong currents, even though on more than one occasion they brought me close to drowning. I persevered until I could swim safely to the bank on the other side. Sometimes I would lie there wet and cold until I regained my strength for the return journey, but I was never deterred.

I began to spar with other cats until they reacted and started a fight. I revelled in the fact that I could subdue but not hurt, crush but not kill.

After a while they seemed to enjoy competing with me. Everywhere I went there were cats prepared to struggle, as much as to gauge their own strength, I suspected, as mine.

Day after day I trained, fiercely and relentlessly, determined to let nothing conquer me. When my strength began to exceed even Li Ming's, other cats began looking at me with respect. By now I had grown big with a thick coat of soft fur that hid my hard muscular body. My whiskers were long and sensitive and Saraha told me that my sapphire-blue eyes had such depth and intensity she could tell that every cat was wary of me.

Even Li Ming knew that my ability was now much greater than his. And it was just possible, all the cats agreed, that some day I might indeed leave home and venture into the unknown.

Anxious though I was to set off on my voyage of discovery, I waited until I felt strong in mind as well as powerful in body. Each day I would spend time in my special tree. In the quietness I was constantly aware of the presence of my ancestor which built up the confidence needed for my journey.

There was no further sign, but within me I had a dedication so intense, so buoyant and so potent that I was capable of pursuing my dream alone.

CONVINCED THAT THE DAY HAD COME, I farewelled my family with emotion.

Karissima licked my head as she'd done when I was a kitten. "I wish you a safe and happy journey," she said fondly, "but I fear for you, Lao-Tsun."

"Have no fear, mother," I replied confidently. "Sinh, who is in paradise, will protect me and keep me safe."

THE JOURNEY

"So be it," said Li Ming. "You also go with our love and our pride, Lao-Tsun, for your dream has become ours." I treasured my father's blessing.

Saraha accompanied me at the start of the journey, then she too bade me farewell. "May our sacred ancestor be with you always, my beloved brother," she said. We looked deeply into each other's eyes, then with just a moment's hesitation, I leapt away at speed to cover as much ground as possible before nightfall.

At the beginning of the journey I was nervous, not knowing what to expect, but became bolder as I moved from one landscape, one country to another.

As I travelled through small towns and villages, the cats were friendly. As they frolicked and played they would often call out to me, "Hi! Stranger! We're going hunting. Come and join us."

Sometimes I longed to but knew that to complete my journey I must keep moving.

But it felt good to be near them. The world is a happy place, I thought.

I hurried on, asking always, "Where is Burma?"

One day in a remote land I asked the question of a small honey-coloured cat. "Why do you want to go to Burma?" she asked.

"I have this dream of a far-away land," I replied, "where my sacred ancestors lived. I have to go there to prove to myself and all Birmans that the legend we have been told about them is really true."

"But that's all it is – a dream," she said softly. "Why waste your life, Lao-Tsun? Stay here with me and we'll raise a family."

Looking into her gentle face and pleading eyes I was sorely tempted. But I thought of my father and my commitment to Sinh and I knew I could not stay.

"Come with me, Asmara," I said.

She shook her head. "That is not my destiny. But may your dream come true, Lao-Tsun."

Sadly, I went on my way - alone once more.

I came to dread the cities and tried to avoid them. The cats there were different from the ones in the country. They gave me cold, hard stares and made aggressive movements towards me with ears flattened and tails lashing. Although I was large and strong, it still took all my courage to go among them.

In one big, crowded city I got lost. What frightened me most was that among all the noise and the dirt I became disorientated – and panicked. I couldn't even hold on to the thought of Sinh and felt completely vulnerable.

I knew I had to get out of there as quickly as possible. I went up to a couple of belligerent-looking cats and asked the way.

"I wouldn't tell you even if I could," replied one rudely.

The other looked at me with an odd expression on his face. "I will," he said in a sly tone, and pointed to an alley. "Just ask for Big George."

I thanked him politely but felt uneasy when I saw the malicious looks they gave each other as I turned away.

Too late, I saw Big George watch me enter his territory. The massive cat had the most evil eyes of any I had ever seen. Sitting up, he yelled to his gang. "Get him!"

Suddenly from nowhere, cats answered their leader's command. They formed into a menacing group, quickly surrounded me - and pounced.

The nightmare had begun.

I fought as courageously as I could but was against too many. Every time I defended myself and shook off one cat, there was another to attack me.

There were many cats with wounds that night, but when it ended, I myself was bruised and beaten. All I could do was crawl to safety as far away from the alley as possible, and collapse.

The world is very cruel, I thought as I lost consciousness.

It was dawn when I felt life returning. I opened my eyes and was amazed to see another Birman tending my wounds.

There was a halo of golden light around the cat's head. Sinh is with me, I thought, convinced that I had died during the night and gone to paradise.

It was a complete surprise when the cat spoke. In a quiet voice he said, "My name is Kyalami. I'm a Birman, too."

"Then... then... I'm not dead?" I whispered.

"You were very close to death when I found you last night," said Kyalami. "What happened?"

"I was... beaten up... by a gang of cats in an alley," I replied haltingly.

Kyalami was shocked. "What took you to such a dangerous place?"

I hung my head. "I'm not used to the ways... of a big city."

"Well, never go there again," ordered Kyalami. "Now, what is your name and why are you here?"

"My name is Lao-Tsun and I'm on a long journey to find the home of our ancestors, the Sacred Cats of Burma – and the Temple of Lao-Tsun."

"The legend is known to me. I heard about it from my father," said Kyalami, looking at me with interest. "But I've never heard of any Birman who has travelled to Burma."

I laughed ruefully. "I thought I would be the one to go. But it's all over now, Kyalami," I said despairingly.

My new friend tended me until I was well enough to forage for myself and I stayed with him until my wounds had healed.

We had long discussions about the legend and what I should do when I found the temple. I trusted Kyalami so completely that I told him of my experiences among the trees and how I believed that Sinh himself had prepared me for the journey.

Kyalami listened in amazement. "You have obviously been chosen," he said with conviction, "so you must fulfil our ancestor's wish for you."

"You really believe that I should continue my journey?" I said hesitantly.

"Lao-Tsun, you must go," said Kyalami. "For the sake of every Birman you must go and find the Sacred Cats and the Temple of Lao-Tsun. Only you can do it!"

I looked agonisingly at him. "But what if I should fail?"

"You won't fail, Lao-Tsun. Already you've come so far and faced so much danger. You haven't given up in the past - and you will not give up now."

Kyalami's words renewed my spirits and my faith.

After much deliberation, I was convinced that what he said was true.

It was with sadness that I took leave of my friend but, thanks to Kyalami's inspiration and care, I set off with my body healed and my will to succeed as strong as ever.

On and on I went, always moving and asking the question, 'Where is Burma?'

Sometimes I had boundless energy and covered vast distances. At other times I trudged along, weary in mind and body. I suffered in the heat of high summer and often had to rest during the day and travel only at night.

When the cool winds of autumn blew, the journey was easier, although it seemed as though it would never end.

After I'd been travelling for a long time through a range of hills, I came down one day to find a great sea of water. Without thinking, I plunged in as I always had – only to find that there was no bank on the other side to climb up. There was just endless water. Frightened that I might drown, I turned back and swam to where I'd started.

It was winter now and I was chilled and shivering. To get warm I began to run, but was dismayed to find that always in the direction I knew I had to go – there was water. I had to get to the other side but didn't know how I was going to do it, yet everything depended on it.

From one day to another I waited anxiously for a sign - each time to be disappointed. Every night I would dream of my ancestor and my faith in a miracle never wavered, though just surviving was difficult.

Food was scarce and there was little shelter. The wind blew and snow fell. Most of the time I was cold and hungry. I was also in pain as one of my wounds from the fight had opened and was festering. I dragged myself into the hollow of a tree and lay there trying to regain my energy and rid my body of the poison.

I had thought of my family often during my travels, but at that moment was overwhelmed with an intense feeling of homesickness. I longed to be mothered by Karissima and lectured to by Li Ming.

Although I wished desperately to see the rest of my family too, most of all I had a great need to have my sister, Saraha, beside me.

One morning after another turned into night and my homesickness grew. It took possession of me to such an extent that I nearly made the decision to return, no matter how difficult or dangerous the journey might be.

But something held me back. Perhaps it was the thought that they would lose the faith they had in me. Perhaps it was that deep down my dedication to my ancestor was still the strongest force in my life. Whatever the reason, I made the decision to continue my search even if, in the end, that search led to nothing.

I awoke one morning and was amazed to see a boat sail across the water. I'd seen such boats on the river. Was this the sign I'd been waiting for? Cautiously, I climbed a small hill beside the water, crept nearer to the edge and saw the boat come close to the land. What surprised me most was that on the deck a large white cat with grey markings was washing himself.

A thought came to me. If that cat can travel across water – so can I! Anxious to continue my journey, I trembled as I tried to judge how far I would have to leap in order to reach the boat. With a mighty vault, I hurled myself into the air. At my highest point, I felt as though an unseen force was lifting my body even higher, so that my range was just enough for me to land on the deck. Shaken, I lay there gasping for breath.

At the sudden intrusion into his territory, the white cat jumped up, his back arching with fear. He hissed and spat at me. The situation, if it hadn't been so serious, would have looked almost comical. Here we were, two grown cats, in fighting mode – in a boat – on the water!

I had to calm the other cat down, so said quietly, "Don't be alarmed. I have not come to hurt you."

"Who are you?" growled the cat suspiciously. "What are you doing here?"

"I'm on a journey," I told him calmly, "a very important journey - but I have to cross this water. I must get to the other side."

The cat listened warily.

"If you will help me, I will be most grateful," I said, "but I warn you, if you do not, I will fight to complete my mission." My words seemed to stun the cat. He backed away and sat at a safe distance. As we looked at each other, the boat moved and to my intense relief, it began to sail away from the land.

For the entire journey, the white cat and I sat watching each other, each one afraid to relax. Although exhausted, I knew I had to keep awake in case of a sudden attack. There would be no Kyalami to come to my aid this time. When I saw green fields coming closer, I gave thanks to Sinh for his deliverance.

I was about to leap overboard when the white cat said gruffly, "I don't know who you are – but I wish you good fortune on your journey."

"Thank you," I replied warmly, "and I shall always remember you with gratitude."

I peered down and saw that I would have to swim the final distance to the shore, but I jumped into the water confident that I could do so. Again I was conscious of a guiding force helping me. As I pulled myself from the water and lay panting on the sand, a surge of excitement and deep satisfaction flowed through me. I had accomplished the impossible – or what had seemed like the impossible

only a short time ago. But I knew that without my ancestor's guidance it could not have happened.

After resting for a while, I began hunting for food to replenish my strength for the long trek ahead. The journey began again, taking me from lush pastures to baked and barren ground where little grew. I became foot sore and was forced to stop for several days until I was healed again. Needing to rest but afraid of dangers on the ground, I climbed a large tree and curled up among its branches.

As I lay there, between sleep and awareness, my mind slowly filled with a soft light of many colours which seemed to glow around me. For the first time

I was also conscious of an image. It came only fleetingly, but I sensed that the intense sapphire-blue eyes, with dark, expanded pupils that looked into mine were indeed those of my ancestor - and I knew for certain I was not alone.

With renewed energy, I made my way across a plateau with little vegetation. Looking around I could see no one. Then in the distance I spotted a cat at play. Coming nearer I called out, "Greetings to you! May I ask a question?"

"Of course," replied the saucy little black and white cat, "though I warn you, I may not know the answer!"

"Where is Burma?"

"Oh, I know that," said the cat as he pranced in and out of a pile of straw. "You go straight ahead." As I thanked him and began to run, the cat shouted, "Wait! I'm wrong. You go right." He thought for a moment, then added, "No. I tell a lie. For Burma, you must turn left."

"Thank you," I said again and hurried on, unaware that the cat's directions were not correct.

Leaving even villages behind, I climbed higher and higher. It was so steep, I became exhausted. When I stopped and looked around, I found myself alone in the vastness of the mountains. I realised I was lost. A desperate loneliness overwhelmed me – and I wept.

"Why are you crying?" a voice asked.

"Because I'm lost and alone," I replied.

"You are not lost," said an impressive looking cat with large blue eyes, "you are in the Himalayas. And you are not alone because I – Sharella – am with you. Tell me why you've come."

The large cat exuded so much warmth and friendliness that soon I found myself explaining about my search for the Sacred Cats and the experiences I'd already had. "Where is Burma?" I asked.

"That I do not know," said Sharella. "But you are in dangerous country, my friend. Many have tried to find their way among our mountains but few have lived to reach the other side."

As we stood together, I looked around and became aware of the utter silence that surrounded us. "How do you live in this quietness?" I asked in a low voice. "Do you ever get lonely?"

Sharella shook her head. "No," she said. "Where there is silence the heart is at peace. And when the heart is at peace, you are as one with the universe." I looked into her wise eyes and knew that she, too, spoke the truth. "This temple of yours," inquired Sharella, "is it worth getting yourself lost and maybe killed for?"

"The purpose of my life is to find the temple," I explained. "If I die before I get there, that means that I was not meant to find such a sacred place." I paused, and then with total conviction added, "but I know within me that I will find it – and the dwelling place of my ancestor, Sinh, in paradise."

Sharella looked at me with admiration. "In that case," she said, "I must help you. I shall lead you out of the mountains."

I put complete trust in Sharella and followed her closely. Finally we emerged from the great mountain range and I was able to continue my journey.

Wearily, I kept travelling.

When I saw two cats conversing, I asked, "Is this... Burma?" An elegant short-haired cat, with markings similar to my own, turned to his friend and said haughtily, "Is that cat addressing us?" Arrogantly, the other replied, "Doesn't he know that Siamese never speak to strangers!' They turned their backs on me and continued their conversation.

As my energy was low, I left them and stumbled on, dazed and without direction until, overcome with tiredness, I fell into a dreamless sleep. When I awoke, a cat, whose fur appeared almost blue in the sunlight, was looking at me with curiosity. Confused, I asked, "Where am I?"

"In Burma," replied the cat. Then he said, "Excuse me, but are you a Sacred Cat?"

I jumped up. "You know of the Sacred Cats?"

"Of course," replied the Burmese, "the Temple of Lao-Tsun is nearby."

The Temple of Lao-Tsun! Hearing those words was joy to my ears. At the same time they filled me with a sense of wonder as I realised that at last my long journey was over.

*a*FTER MUCH SEARCHING, I FOUND IT. The underground temple was in a cave surrounded by heavy vegetation and I crept towards it. This was the moment I had desired so passionately for so long. It seemed almost unbelievable that I was actually in Burma, at the entrance to the temple that held all my dreams.

THE LEGEND

Fascinated, I gazed into it and wondered what mysteries it held. I moved closer but was stopped by a temple guard.

"Leave our sacred temple!" he yelled.

He frightened me, but I stood my ground and replied, "But I'm a Birman."

"Birman you may be. Sacred Birman you are not!" The guard lunged at me, fury in his eyes.

I fell back shouting, "I must speak with a Sacred Cat!"

To my amazement, a calm voice replied, "Speak!"

I turned, bewildered, for I could see no one. Then I looked up into a tree above and saw a large, noble Birman studying me.

"I am Sinh, direct descendant of our illustrious ancestor," said the cat in an authoritative voice. "Why do you invade our temple?"

Bowing slightly before such a majestic presence, I replied humbly, "It was not my intention to invade it. My name is Lao-Tsun. I am called after the temple and have travelled the world to find it."

"Why did you make such a journey?" asked Sinh.

"To find the home of my ancestors – the Temple of Lao-Tsun – and the Sacred Cats," I replied.

Sinh waited, his dark sapphire-blue eyes studying me intently. I was too much in awe of him to speak again. Then he dismissed me, saying, "And now you have found us, go home, little cat."

Shattered, I cried, "I can't go home. I want to be with you – to become a Sacred Cat. Please let me stay."

"No," Sinh said decisively. "We do not accept strangers." And he vanished.

Devastated, I turned away. To have come so far and be rejected was something I had never thought possible. My dream has ended I thought, and lying down fell into a distressed sleep.

Then out of the darkness, an image came to me. Clearly I saw my ancestor. I felt his presence and sensed that I had neither been betrayed nor rejected.

Suddenly, I was filled with a new sense of purpose. The journey was over. I was in Burma, had found the temple – and spoken with Sinh's descendant. I was not going to be defeated by one refusal. There must be a way to become a Sacred Cat.

When I heard someone call my name, I was too involved in my own thoughts to answer. It came again. I turned my head. To my surprise, a small cat came up to me.

"My name is Little Sinh," whispered the kitten. "Don't give up, Lao-Tsun. Because you are not one of us you wouldn't know that unless you are born a Sacred Cat – you have to pass a test to join us."

"Pass a test?" I repeated.

"Yes," said Little Sinh, "but under our law, unless you ask for it, it will not be given to you. Go again to my father."

I looked into the face of Sinh's little son and thought in wonderment that my prayer had been answered. A surge of hope flooded over me as together we went in search of Sinh.

He was sitting among a group of Sacred Cats. I went to him and said formally, "As a stranger, Sinh, I request the opportunity to be tested for the great honour of becoming a Sacred Cat. Will you consider me?"

This time, Sinh looked kindly on me as he granted my request. "We need Birmans such as you," he said. "The number of our Temple Cats has dwindled, but I warn you, Lao-Tsun, the task I shall set you has been attempted many times but no cat has yet succeeded."

"I pray to our ancestors that I shall be the one to succeed," I said passionately.

"Come with me," ordered Sinh, and he led me through the undergrowth. When we reached a small clearing, he stopped. "This is where your task will take place," he said, pointing to a heavily barred cage.

"You will be locked inside.

"You must get out by yourself.

"No one may help you.

"Should you fail – you will die.

"But if you succeed – you will truly become a Sacred Cat."

I stared into the cage and wondered if I was equal to the task.

Sinh knew I was in turmoil for he said gently, "There is still time to make up your mind. Think about what I have said. I will come in the morning for your answer."

All night long, visions came to me. I saw my father, Li Ming, saying, "Honour our ancestors always." I heard Asmara's farewell, "May your dream come true, Lao-Tsun," and deep within myself I yearned to fulfil my life's desire.

When the inspirational words of Kyalami came to me, "Only you can do it!" I knew I had to try.

Sinh welcomed my decision and I was led to the cage and told to enter. When the door was locked behind me, I sat quietly, waiting anxiously to see what would happen next.

A horn sounded and all the Sacred Cats, led by Sinh, walked around the clearing. They surrounded me and sat, silently waiting.

I put my ears back and stalked around the cage. It was small and its bars were strong. They seemed to be crowding in on me.

Suddenly I panicked and ran from side to side, tearing and pulling at the bars. They were rough and tore my paws.

The Sacred Cats, their coats golden in the sunlight, watched impassively. I lay down, licked my wounds and tried to calm myself.

I prayed to my ancestor, "Help me, Sinh." When no response came, I realised that I had to endure – and conquer – the test by myself. I had to prove I was worthy of being a Sacred Cat. Rising slowly, I used all my strength to force the bars apart – but could not. I pushed again and again.

By midday the sun was overhead. I longed for a drink but knew that no one would come to me. Once more I threw myself against the bars – and fell back exhausted.

Because I had no idea of what was expected of me, I decided to conserve my energy, so tucking my paws under my body I tried to sleep. Although sleep would not come, after a time I felt more relaxed and able to cope with the searing heat. Still the Sacred Cats sat watching me, but I drew little comfort from their presence.

As the day cooled and turned into evening, my strength returned. Pacing the cage again and again I tried every means I could think of to force open the door. No matter how hard I tried or how many times I attempted to win my freedom, everything failed.

I was completely trapped and conscious that my energy was ebbing swiftly. The anguish of failure was more than I could bear. Drifting into short bursts of tortured sleep, I felt terribly alone. The night seemed as though it would never end.

Eventually, the morning dawned and with it renewed hope. After all my failed attempts to leave the cage, I now realised that strength alone was not the answer. There must be another way - but what?

As the sun burned through that long, exhausting day, I sat like a statue pondering this seemingly inexplicable question. My thirst was almost unbearable. I lay down and stretched my body across the floor of the cage. Slowly, as though being drawn into a state of oblivion, sleep overcame me but it was not a peaceful sleep.

Dreams came quickly then vanished, each one more unsettling than the last. I was taken back to some of the most horrifying events of my journey. I was fighting for my life in the big city again, getting lost, almost drowning. The last dream turned into a nightmare filled with so much fear and anguish that I was left trembling violently, waves of nausea sweeping over me.

It was almost dark when I awoke and lay there, exhausted, unable to move. I'm dying, I thought.

Through half-closed eyes I saw the Sacred Cats conferring. When Sinh came close to the cage, although in agony, I struggled to my feet to pay him homage.

"Your time is now short in this world, Lao-Tsun," said Sinh. "Under normal circumstances we would let you die. But you have already shown so much courage and determination during your long and arduous journey to reach the Temple of Lao-Tsun, we will allow you to go free. However," Sinh added with regret, "you will not become a Sacred Cat." He went to open the cage door.

"No!" I cried. "Leaving the cage without becoming a Sacred Cat would mean defeat and that I could not endure."

With a surge of energy flowing through me, I straightened up and holding myself erect, spoke with conviction. "I did not come here to fail. I came to be accepted as a Sacred Cat with our ancestor as my guide. I will stay within the cage."

"I accept your decision," said Sinh quietly and returned to his place.

I looked from one Sacred Cat to another. Although they returned my gaze with inscrutable eyes, I felt they were watching me with respect.

As the night became darker, a crescent moon rose high in the sky casting its silver shadows over the clearing. Days without food and water and the intense heat had taken their toll on me.

I found myself slipping back into a torment of suffering and distress. I had endured so much to fulfil my dream, but now began to wonder if I would live long enough to prove that I had the qualities needed to be a Sacred Cat.

Against my will I found myself doubting my own worthiness. But even in the midst of my despair I knew I had to fight this devastating and destructive reaction.

Closing my eyes, I created an image of my ancestor enveloped in brilliant blue light just as he had come to me when I was a kitten. The image was so strong and its effect so healing, I was able, with great effort, to dismiss the negative force that had almost destroyed me.

At that moment I laid aside all my personal hopes and dreams. I had done everything within my power to become a Sacred Cat and failed. This must mean that I was not meant to become one and would die without fulfilling my deepest desire. But if that was to be my fate, I would accept it.

I experienced a sense of release with this decision and

was at peace with myself. In that instant I offered my soul to my ancestor in paradise.

For the first time since entering the cage, I fell into a relaxed and tranquil sleep that seemed to soothe not only my body but my tortured mind.

On wakening, I sensed there was another presence inside the cage. It was so powerful I knew this was not in my imagination but was truly my ancestor. I focussed on the large deep sapphire-blue eyes that seemed to fill the cage with their intensity. I was alone no longer.

The fact that my ancestor was with me at this time was an honour beyond price. If this was to be my final moment, I would die in the knowledge that all I had suffered was not in vain.

Then I became aware of a sound – a deep, primordial humming. It sent waves of vibrations through my aching body, forcing me back to life.

My entire being was pervaded with a consciousness that seemed to wash away all my pain and my fear. With it came a healing of body and mind and soul that left me almost drunk from the rapture within.

As I grew stronger, I opened my eyes and realised that the sound was coming from Sinh and the Sacred Cats, whose eyes were blazing with a supernatural glow just like those of my ancestor.

I stared at them in wonder. Although so still, they radiated a spiritual quality that transcended their physical bodies.

They're in a state of ecstasy, I thought, and was overcome with sadness that I was not one with them.

Suddenly to my amazement, I saw a brilliant light flow directly from my ancestor's eyes into my own.

I became breathless and was bathed in a radiance that became as deeply blue as the eyes of my beloved Sinh. A great warmth spread through me and I experienced a feeling of such joy I felt I was floating.

My desire to become a Sacred Cat returned so intensely that my spirit soared and I, too, entered their timeless world of ecstasy.

I drifted into a sensation of divine happiness and felt myself being lovingly embraced by my ancestor. Becoming one with him brought me to a state of perfect bliss.

At that moment I knew I was in paradise.

How long I remained there I do not know, but gradually realised that the Sacred Cats were stirring and moving closer.

Even before I heard Little Sinh call out, "The cage door is opening!" I sensed that through the grace of my ancestor, I had willed myself free.

My happiness knew no bounds for my dream had come true.

In the midst of rejoicing, my first thought was to give thanks to my ancestor and the Sacred Cats. I also blessed my family and all those whose love and support had helped me achieve the seemingly impossible.

I was now a Sacred Cat myself and would live in the Temple of Lao-Tsun until I was called to remain with my ancestor in paradise forever.

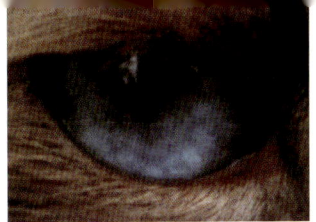

*F*ROM THE MOMENT LAO-TSUN WAS CREATED
a Sacred Cat, news of his exploits flowed from cat to cat.

Across valleys, plains and mountains.

Through villages, towns and cities.

From one country to another.

From one continent to the next.

EPILOGUE

North – south – east – west – until it encircled the globe.

They told of his determination, his daring – his dream.

They marvelled that he had made it all come true.

They told it with pride, with joy and with love,

for this was above rivalry, jealousy and hate.

Every cat, from the pampered to the poorest,

was enriched by the magic of Lao-Tsun,

for he had become a legend in his own lifetime.

The day I saw my first Birman cat and looked into his deep sapphire blue eyes, I was enchanted and determined to have a Birman of my own. Within a few weeks I had one - a blue point Birman kitten.

When my cat was about one year old, Denese Moore, a friend and professional photographer, saw him and she, too, was captivated. It was her

AUTHORS NOTE

suggestion that she photograph him that gave me the idea to write a book.

When looking for a theme, I studied the legend of the Birmans and felt that I could include it. The fact that they are known as the Sacred Cats of Burma added an extra dimension.

Denese and I spent many hours together as she photographed not only Birmans but other breeds as well, so that I could weave them into the story. We became so obsessed with photographing cats that friends called us the 'Mad Catters'! It was a real labour of love for Denese and myself as we are both ardent cat lovers.

Because my cat was already too old to be photographed in the 'kitten' sequence, we went back to Dhyama Cattery where I had bought mine, and were lucky enough to find that a new litter of eight-week-old kittens had been born to the same mother and father as my cat. This meant that we could start the story when Lao-Tsun was a kitten.

When Lao-Tsun was old enough to go on his journey, my own cat took over as the leading character and you'll see many photographs of him looking quite magnificent.

Although, with the legend, I had the basis of a story, it didn't really develop until the young cats were photographed. With the pictures in front of me, I began to shuffle them around, looking for certain expressions and 'body language'. Bit by bit I began to develop a story line that took Lao-Tsun from the earliest days through his discovery of the legend and the response he got when he told all his friends how wonderful the Birmans were! For this, Denese captured the pathetic-looking wet cat in a cave that calls Lao-Tsun a snob! It progressed through

to the manifestation of his dream that gave him the will to set off on his adventure.

Denese completed the 'Dream' sequence first and by then I had a definite idea of how he would prepare himself for 'The Journey'.

As many of our friends allowed us to photograph their pets, we were able to include in a variety of poses all kinds of cats from pure bred to attractive 'moggies'. Denese has such an amazing affinity with animals, she was able to capture the most incredible pictures. One I always enjoy looking at is the sly-looking cat pointing down the dark alley with his paw across his body.

After photographing the gang leader, 'Big George', he needed a gang. We went to various destination looking for wild cats until we found a group with that tough, determined look in their eyes - the ones who are out to get Lao-Tsun.

As the story progressed, I was able to visualise how the legend could become part of 'The Sacred Cat'. When Lao-Tsun arrives at the home of the Sacred Cats and is given the opportunity to take the test to become a Sacred Cat himself, it was another challenge for us to show how it could be done.

Photographing Lao-Tsun in the cage was a time of extreme patience for Denese. My cat acted superbly but she had to capture his many moods, from panic to near death. The final pictures of him as a Sacred Cat are totally believable. He simply radiates a magic and a spiritual quality seldom seen, even in humans.

The book started off as a simple tale of a young cat who travels the world to find the home of his ancestors in Burma, but has been rewritten many times. I have never before been so passionate about any of my eleven books as I have about 'The Sacred Cat'. It has dominated me since it was conceived. As my own experience deepened and I became aware of meditation and a more spiritual way of life, the story of Lao-Tsun in the re-writing came to mirror my own development and thinking.

Cats are often perceived as spiritual creatures - in some countries they are treated as gods - and it seemed only natural that Lao-Tsun should be influenced and guided by his ancestor, Sinh, who in the legend had gone to paradise when he died.

So, in time, "The Sacred Cat" became an allegory - the ability of an individual to overcome seemingly impossible odds. Now that it is completed, many people read more into the story than the adventure of a cat. About two months after the photography was completed, my beautiful Birman was killed on the road outside my home. When I look at his grave under a tree in my garden, I can't help feeling that he came into this world for a purpose. If that purpose is to inspire us with the story of Lao Tsun, then he could well be happy in his final resting place - perhaps in paradise with his ancestor.

Marie Stuttard

THE AUTHOR

Marie Stuttard

Marie Stuttard is an international author and speaker, who has been broadcasting on radio and television for many years with the B.B.C. and in New Zealand. She has a teacher's diploma from the Guildhall School of Speech and Drama, London, and is a corporate lecturer on speech and communication, specialising in 'Power of Speech' seminars.

Her Internet site – http://www.speechpower.co.nz features her books, 'The Power of Speech' and 'The Power of Public Speaking' published by Batemans. The books are also published in the United States and Canada by Barrons. Her site includes her own audio and video cassettes.

Several of Marie's eleven books were written for children. These include titles such as 'Children of the Dog Star', which became a television series and 'The Boy from Nowhere', an unusual and mystical story set in her home city of Auckland.

She has been a journalist, fashion editor of Vogue New Zealand and has had her own publicity business.

Marie was born in Ireland but has lived in New Zealand for many years. She has one daughter, Liz, and two grandchildren, Claire and Louise and a Swiss 'adopted' daughter, Carol, who lives nearby. Carol was a real support in the preparation of this book. Marie's constant companions are Misty, a German Shepherd, and Neptune, a Rottweiler cross, who are also part of her much loved family!

THE PHOTOGRAPHER

Denese Moore

Denese Moore is one of New Zealand's most experienced photographers. After training and tutoring in photography, she joined the School of Architecture, University of Auckland, New Zealand. Her contact with staff and students was both challenging and enjoyable. This included photography, tutoring, displays and illustrating lectures.

After twenty years at the university she opened a photographic business with her daughter, Kerrie, called "Top Cat Photography"! Kerrie has carried on into television and video production.

Denese's love of animals is obvious in her superb photography. Commissions to photograph animals are what she finds most creatively rewarding and tend to dominate her portfolio. However, when illustrating a book about hang gliding once, she vividly remembers racing up and down steep hills to get the photographs she needed!

Other memorable assignments include bobbing in boats and hanging from helicopters to record some fabulous estates in Australia and New Zealand. Her clients later used her photographs in a variety of overseas magazines and books.

Denese's portraits of many people, including those from overseas, are still being requested for inclusion in major publications.

She has a Jack Russell terrier called 'Zo'. Her loved cat, 'Muffy' (the one seen laughing in the book) has died but she shares other cats with her neighbours.

ACKNOWLEDGEMENTS

- The book got off to a wonderful start thanks to Barbara and Ian Dutton. They welcomed us into their home where so many of the photographs of Birmans were taken. All these cats were from Dhyana Cattery, where the registered breeders are their son and daughter, Antony and Angela Dutton.

- All those who allowed us to photograph their cats - Jill Calveley, Avelyn Davidson, Fran Elkin, Pat and Lesley Fallon, Beverley Hill, Mary Lou Hudson, Philip Nolloth, Joan Ready, Sue and Karen, and Doreen Townley – with a special thanks to Barbara and Bruce Herrick who also allowed us to use a photograph of their cat, Sharella.

- Photograph on Page 4 - Frankie Euphrate

- Many Birman breeders including Julie Johnson and Lee Williams.

- Catherine McDonald, managing director of Book Lovers International, for her vision and commitment to the book and her continuous input which has contributed so much to its success.

- David Guthrie of G. M. Media for his initial decision to publish the book, which led to the formation of Sacred Cats Ltd. with Marie and Denise, and for his tireless and inspired leadership.

- The professionalism and creativity of the design and production team: Stan Tucker of HotHouse Design Group Ltd; Jonathan Guthrie and Alexandra Robinson of Digital River Ltd.

- Shirley Forde for all her help with promotions and publicity.

- Bob Kerridge, Executive Director of the Auckland S.P.C.A. for his constant support.

THE Sacred CAT

Published by:	Sacred Cat Ltd, PO Box 25 667, Auckland, New Zealand
Publishing Editor:	David Guthrie
Publishing support:	GM Media Ltd, Auckland Book Lovers International Ltd, Auckland
Design:	Stan Tucker, HotHouse Design Group Ltd, Auckland
Layout and Pre-Press:	Jonathan Guthrie, Alexandra Robinson and Simon Harris, Digital River Ltd, Auckland
Scans and Film:	Digital River Ltd, Auckland
Plates:	Crosspoint Litho Ltd, Auckland
Printing:	Impex Press (NZ) Ltd, Auckland
Text:	Marie Stuttard
Photography:	Denese Moore
Email:	info@sacredcat.co.nz
Internet Website:	http://www.sacredcat.co.nz